In memory of Debbie B.
— J.S.

For Arfi
— N.A.

Clarion Books is an imprint of HarperCollins Publishers.
First Day, Hooray!
Copyright © 2024 by HarperCollins Publishers
All rights reserved. Manufactured in Italy. No part of this book may be used or reproduced in any manner whatsoever
without written permission except in the case of brief quotations embodied in critical articles and reviews. For information
address HarperCollins Children's Books, a division of HarperCollins Publishers, 195 Broadway, New York, NY 10007.
www.harpercollinschildrens.com

Library of Congress Control Number: 2023943878
ISBN 978-0-06-326578-3
The artist used Adobe Photoshop to create the digital illustrations for this book.
Typography by Phil Caminiti and Honee Jang
24 25 26 27 28 RTLO 10 9 8 7 6 5 4 3 2 1

First Edition

FIRST DAY, HOORAY!

BY **June Sobel**   ILLUSTRATED BY **Nabila Adani**

Clarion Books
An Imprint of HarperCollinsPublishers

Off we go! Hooray! Hooray!
A new school year begins today.

First day is here. Give a shout!
Take a breath. Breathe in. Breathe out.

Excited, nervous, a little scared.
Are we ready? All prepared?

Backpacks filled with school supplies,
but something else hides in disguise!

Out of sight and stashed away,
feelings visit us all day.

They swirl around, fast or slow.
Find their names and say "hello!"

Hello **HAPPY** soaring by.
A joyful bird loves to fly!

Hey there, **WORRY**. That's OK.

School is cool. I want to stay.

What's up, **ANGER**? Take time out.
Tame the flame. Breathe in. Breathe out.

Feelings are not right or wrong.
They find a spot where they belong.

Pull out **BRAVE**. Take a chance!

Go on stage! Sing and dance!

Art time is here.
Let's find a chair!

EMBARRASSED!

Oops! Paint in my hair!

Uh oh, **SCARED**, lunch line is slow.
Where's my table, a friend I know?

Take a breath. Breathe in. Breathe out.
You'll find a spot without a doubt.

EXCITED leaps! Playground fun!

Bouncing balls! It's time to run!

Broke my pencil. Lost my folder.

MAD sulks. Tempers smolder.

Take a breath. Close your eyes.
Pretend to float. Let CALM arise.

CURIOUS questions, asking why

flowers grow
and birds can fly.

Wow! **SuRPRISE!** We are all done.

Pack up your feelings one by one.

Time to go! Oh, what a day!

One feeling's left. And it's HOORAY!

When children begin school, they may experience many things: learning routines, forming friendships, trying new skills, or making mistakes. They may also feel a range of emotions, from fear, worry, and anger to surprise, bravery, and excitement. Books are a powerful tool for discussing what emotions look like, sound like, and feel like during big transitions, such as starting school.

Teaching children about their emotions empowers them to effectively express and regulate themselves. When children have words for their feelings—*I'm feeling disappointed, I'm feeling frustrated, I'm feeling calm*—it also helps others understand what they're experiencing and how to best support them. Children need to hear from the people in their lives that their emotions matter, that there is no such thing as a good or bad emotion, and that what they are going through is normal.

WHILE YOU READ:

- Explore the emotional clues on each page and ask questions: "What feelings do you notice?" "How do you know a character is feeling a certain way?" "What happened to make them feel that way?"

- Help your child understand that their emotions matter by encouraging them to imagine their own first day of school: "How do you think you will feel at school?" "What do you do when you're feeling excited?" "What could you do if you're feeling scared at school?"

- Show them that a range of feelings are normal by sharing your own experiences: "I feel happy when . . ." "When I'm angry, I raise my voice." "What is something I could do if I'm feeling frustrated and want to calm my body?"

- Less is more—don't ask too many questions! Select a few emotions to discuss each time you read. Be sure to discuss both pleasant and unpleasant feelings.

Sharing emotional experiences through storytelling is a fun and helpful way to make sure children feel safe, curious, and calm when facing a big milestone. Learning that everyone experiences many emotions when they start something new will help them feel confidence and a sense of belonging at school.

Craig S. Bailey, PhD
Director of Early Childhood, Yale Center for Emotional Intelligence
Assistant Professor, Yale Child Study Center